MW01121977

A Birthday Basket for Tía

by Pat Mora
illustrated by Cecily Lang

Book Guide

SNAPSHOTS
Grade 2, Unit 1

Cover from A BIRTHDAY BASKET FOR TÍA by Pat Mora, illustrated by Cecily Lang. Illustration copyright © 1992 by Cecily Lang.
Published by Macmillan Publishing Company. Photograph of Pat Mora courtesy of Valerie Santagto. © Santagto for Scholastic Inc.

Contents

Dear Teacher,

A *Birthday Basket for Tía* celebrates the special bond between a little girl and her great-aunt. The first person text and the vibrant illustrations help readers share in Cecilia's enthusiasm as she prepares a very special gift for her beloved Tía Rosa. Through their reading and book conversations children will come to appreciate that it is the little things we do every day that add up to a lifetime of love and memories.

Overview

TEACHING OPTIONS

There are many ways that children can read and enjoy *A Birthday Basket for Tía.*

◆ Almost all children can benefit from having all or part of the book **read aloud** to help them appreciate the dialogue, and the rich language, including the Spanish words. You may wish to have pairs take turns reading the narration and the dialogue. An **audiocassette version** of this story is part of the Trade Book Listening Center.

◆ A reading plan that uses the **key strategy** of **Make Predictions** and **Phonics: Vowel /a/a (-and, -ank)** and **Vowel /i/i (-int)** balances **teacher guidance** with **demonstrating independence.** This option has children reading portions of the book on their own and then participating in teacher-led discussion to stimulate **meaningful conversation** and comprehension. See Reading the Book pages 6-7. This plan may be used for **whole class** or **cooperative group** instruction.

◆ Children may also read **independently** or in **pairs.**

◆ Introducing the Book, Assess Comprehension, Writing, Activities, and the Story Organizer are features of this guide that may be used with all children.

CONNECT TO SOURCEBOOK

Resources in the *Snapshots* **Teacher's SourceBook**, such as lessons relating to the key strategy of Make Predictions and the Phonics: Vowel /a/a (-and, -ank),and Vowel /i/i (-int) may also be adapted for use with *A Birthday Basket for Tía.*

In addition, each plan in the *Snapshots* Teacher's SourceBook includes **specific suggestions for linking *A Birthday Basket for Tía* to the SourceBook literature**. Detailed suggestions are provided on pages **T253** and **T301** of the Teacher's SourceBook and on page **8** of this guide. Additional suggestions appear on pages T39,T91, T155, and T203 of the Teacher's SourceBook.

PHONICS PRACTICE

This guide **highlights Vowel /a/ a (-and, -ank)** and **Vowel /i/i (-int)**. The lesson on page 6 allows children to review and expand their knowledge of short vowel sounds as they decode and make new words with these phonograms.

JOURNAL WRITING

Throughout *Literacy Place* children use journal writing to record their observations, note new vocabulary, express their imaginations, and link reading to real-life experiences. Within this guide **opportunities** for journal writing are found on pages **4, 5,** and **7.**

PORTFOLIO ASSESSMENT

This guide offers a number of opportunities for portfolio assessment of both reading and writing.

WRITING
See pages 10-11.

READING
See pages 8-9, 12.

Introducing the Book

CREATE INTEREST

Spark children's interest by asking them to describe birthday presents they have given to family members. How did they decide what to give? Did they buy or make the gift? What help did they give with the gift? Write children's responses on the chalkboard.

BUILD BACKGROUND

Tell children that the book they will read is about a girl who wants to give her great-aunt a special birthday present. Explain that in Spanish, the word for *aunt* is *tía*. (The word for *uncle* is *tío*.) Invite a volunteer to explain how an aunt is related to you. (She is the sister of your mother or father.) Then help children understand that your *great-aunt* is a sister of any of your grandparents.

Vocabulary

Story Words

mixing bowl: a bowl used for mixing food (p. 12)

sugary: having a lot of sugar (p.12)

dough: soft, thick mix of flour and water (p.12)

refrigerator: large holder that keeps food cold (p. 22)

musicians: people who play music (p. 26)

guitars: musical instruments with six strings that are plucked with fingers (p. 26)

violins: stringed instruments played with bows (p. 26)

DEVELOP VOCABULARY

Strategy: Semantic Map

Write the first four story words on the chalkboard. Read them aloud and then have children read each one with you and talk about its meaning.

Begin a word web on the chalkboard with *dough* in the center. As you add *sugary, mixing bowl,* and *refrigerator* to the web, ask children to tell how each of these words is related to *dough*. Then call on volunteers to add other words to the web and explain how each is related to dough. Repeat the procedure with *musicians, guitars,* and *violins*.

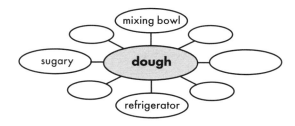

Personal Word List Encourage children to generate their own lists of words relating to dough or musicians and other words they find interesting as they read the book.

Support Words You may wish to review the support words listed below before children read *A Birthday Basket for Tía.*

bubbling: rising in bubbles (p.7)

perfume: sweet-smelling oil worn on the body (p.10)

flowerpot: pot for holding flowers (p.14)

braids: hair tied in twists (p.18)

PREVIEW AND PREDICT

Display the front cover of *A Birthday Present for Tía* and ask children to tell what they see. Read aloud the book title and the names of the author and illustrator.

Have children page through the book to look for words that appear in slanted print, or italics. Explain that those words are Spanish words. Why might the author use Spanish words in her story?

Before children begin reading ask what they think will happen in the story. You may wish to use the following questions as prompts.

◆ **What do you think the birthday basket for Tía will have in it?**

◆ **What do you think Tía will do or say after she receives the basket?**

Invite children to record their predictions about the story in their Journals. As they read, children can see how their predictions compare to what actually happens in the story.

ASSESSMENT

As children read the book, notice how they:

✔ make connections to the **theme** of what our actions tell about us.

✔ use the **key strategy** of Make Predictions.

✔ **compare** and **contrast** characters to better understand the story.

✔ use **phonics** including Vowel /a/a (*and, ank*) and /i/i (*int*).

Meet the Author

Pat Mora based *A Birthday Basket for Tía* on her childhood experiences in the Mexican-American community of El Paso, where she grew up. She is a prominent poet whose work had been published in three collections of her own writing as well as in anthologies and textbooks. In addition to writing poetry, Ms. Mora has written several children's books. She is the recipient of a Kellogg National Fellowship, and has also worked as a teacher. *A Birthday Basket for Tía* received the Southwest Book Award in 1992.

MORE BOOKS BY PAT MORA

***A Birthday Basket for Tía*
Trade Book Listening Center**
This audiocassette offers another way to enjoy this book.

Una canasta para Tía
This Spanish language version of *A Birthday Basket for Tía* is just as much fun as the English version.

Pablo's Tree
Pablo's grandfather planted a tree on the day Pablo was adopted and became part of his family.

The Desert Is My Mother
This poetic book recreates one girl's wonder for the desert in both English and Spanish.

The Race of Toad and Deer
This folktale from Guatemala has been retold by Pat Mora with humor and suspense.

Reading the Book

MINI-LESSON

PHONICS:
Vowel /a/a
(-and, -ank),
Vowel /i/i (-int)

TEACH/MODEL On the chalkboard, write these sentences: I draw pictures in the sand. "Chica, shall we give her little pots, my piggy bank?" Read the sentences aloud with children. Underline the words *sand* and *bank*. Ask children to say these words again and listen for the short *a* sound in each one. Then repeat the procedure for the following sentence and the short *i* sound: My aunt makes me hot mint tea.

APPLY On the chalkboard write the phonograms *-and, -ank,* and *-int*. Invite volunteers to come to the chalkboard and add consonants to the beginning of each phonogram to make new words.

Phonics

Synopsis   A girl named Cecilia prepares a gift basket for her great-aunt's ninetieth birthday. While her cat looks on, Cecilia includes items she and Tía use when they spend time together: a book, mixing bowl, flowerpot, teacup, red ball, and flowers. Tía is pleased with her surprise party and present.

LAUNCH THE KEY STRATEGY
MAKE PREDICTIONS

THINK ALOUD   When I read a story, I look for clues in the words and pictures to figure out what might happen. I also use what I already know and my experience to help me make predictions. From the cover of this book I can tell that the girl and the older woman are very happy together. The title tells me that it is Tía's birthday. I know that tía means aunt in Spanish, so Tía is probably the older woman in the picture. The streamers in the picture are another clue that it is a birthday party. I predict that the girl in the picture has given Tía a special birthday present.

COMPREHENSION CHECK
After page 11

Why does Cecilia describe the day as "secret day"? (Make Inferences) *Her great-aunt does not know there will be a surprise party for her.*

What problem does Cecilia have? (Plot) *She doesn't know what to give Tía for a birthday present.*

How does Chica the cat help Cecilia? How does Chica interfere at times? (Summarize) *Chica helped by keeping Cecilia company. She interferes by jumping in the basket and sitting on the book.*

Why does Cecilia choose to put a book in the basket? (Draw Conclusions) *The book is something special that Cecilia and Tía enjoy when they are together.*

What else do you think Cecilia will put into Tía's birthday basket? (Key Strategy: Make Predictions) *Answer will vary. Children may predict that she will put in more items that she and Tía use together.*

After page 21

What other items does Cecilia choose to put in the basket?
(Problem/Solution) *She puts in a mixing bowl, a flowerpot, a teacup, a red ball, and flowers.*

How are Cecilia and her Aunt alike? How are they different?
(Compare/Contrast) *Possible answers include that they are alike in that they like to do things together such as play ball and grow flowers. They are different in that Cecilia is a little girl and her aunt is ninety years old.* `MINI-LESSON`

What do all the items that Cecilia picks for the basket have in common? (Categorize Information) *They are all favorite things that she and Tía enjoy together.*

Which of the items in the basket do you think is the nicest? Why?
(Make Judgments) *Answers will vary.*

How can you tell that Cecilia and Tía love each other? (Character)
Tía does many nice things for Cecilia, such as reading to her, baking cookies with her, playing with her, and caring for her when she's sick. Cecilia wants to make a nice present for Tía.

What do you think Tía will do when she gets Cecilia's basket?
(Key Strategy: Make Predictions) *Answers will vary.*

After page 32

What special things are at the party? (Summarize) *There are musicians, flowers, balloons, tiny cakes, a piñata, and Cecilia's basket.*

How can you tell that Tía likes Cecilia's present?
(Draw Conclusions) *She smiles as she looks at its contents, and danced with Cecilia.*

What does the birthday basket tell you about the kinds of things Cecilia and her great-aunt like to do? (Theme Connection) *The basket shows that they both enjoy many different hobbies.*

What do you think Tía might give as a present on Cecilia's birthday? (Key Strategy: Make Predictions)
Possible answer: She may give items that they can enjoy together.

If you were to give a birthday basket to one of your relatives, what kinds of things would you put in it? Write about these things in your Journal.

MINI-LESSON

COMPARE/CONTRAST

TEACH/MODEL As children read the story have them compare Cecilia and Tía Rosa to each other.

THINK ALOUD As I read a story, I think about the characters and how they are alike and how they are different. At the beginning of the story I learn that Cecilia is a little girl and Tía Rosa is ninety years old. Then I found out that these two like to do many things together.

APPLY Have children go back and look through pages 12-21 to find more ways that Cecilia and her aunt are alike and ways they are different. Encourage them to record the information they find in a chart or Venn diagram.

Assess Comprehension

REFLECT AND RESPOND

Did anything in *A Birthday Basket for Tía* surprise you? What part of the ending were you able to predict? What helped you make your predictions? (✔ Key Strategy: Make Predictions)

How do Tía and Cecilia show that they love each other? (✔ Compare/Contrast)

Mama and Cecilia plan a surprise party for Tía Rosa. What does this tell you about them? (✔ Theme Connection)

How is Tía's birthday celebration like or unlike other birthday parties you've been to? (✔ Respond to Literature)

STORY ORGANIZER

Copy and distribute the Story Organizer on page 12 of this guide. Invite children to complete this page on their own. Encourage them to share their completed work by comparing their answers with those of other children.

CHECK PREDICTIONS

Ask children to return to their Journals and check their predictions to see how well their predictions matched what happened in the story. Have them revise their predictions if necessary.

READ CRITICALLY ACROSS TEXTS: CONNECT TO THE SOURCEBOOK

Ronald Morgan Goes to Bat
◆ Compare and contrast *A Birthday Basket for Tía* with *Ronald Morgan Goes to Bat*. How does the main character in each story show how people help each other?

◆ What do you think Ronald Morgan's teammates would put in a birthday basket for him?

Ruby the Copycat
◆ Compare and contrast the pictures in *A Birthday Basket for Tía* and *Ruby the Copycat*. What do they tell you about the feelings of the characters?

A Topic for Conversation

MORE THAN I CAN SAY

Sometimes a character's actions tell more than any words that the character can say. Discuss that at the end of *A Birthday Basket for Tía*, Cecilia's aunt surprises her by dropping her cane and starting to dance. What does this action say about Tía Rosa and how she is feeling? Invite all those who have read *A Birthday Basket for Tía*, to discuss this question.

POSSIBLE ANSWERS:

Tía Rosa is so happy she feels young again.

Cecilia's present let her know how much Cecilia cares about her. She is so happy she can't even speak.

Tía Rosa is still so surprised she isn't ready to talk yet.

She wants to dance with Cecilia to show her how much she likes her present.

IDEA FILE

Repeated Reading

Partner Reading Children can work with a partner to read the book aloud. Have them take turns reading the narration and Cecilia's monologue to Chica, the cat. Encourage children to read with expression, particularly when reading Cecilia's words.

Listening

Have children listen to the audiocassette noting how the narrator reads with expression to help make clear how Cecilia and others feel as the story progresses. Then invite children to read a part of the book aloud to a partner. Remind them to use expression to help their partner know how the characters feel.

Write a Dialogue

Cecilia imagines what her cat would say if she could talk. Invite children to choose one of the pictures with Chica in it and write what the cat might be thinking in that situation. Encourage children to write a dialogue between Chica and Cecilia.

Vocabulary

Invite children to describe a new activity that Cecilia and Tía might do together the day after Tía's party. Children can work in cooperative groups to write an extension for the book. Encourage them to use as many words from their Personal Word lists as they can.

Piñatas At the surprise party for Tía, there is a piñata—a container made of papier-mâché or clay, and often shaped like an animal. It is filled with fruit, candy, and toys. Piñatas are popular items at Mexican celebrations such as birthday parties and the nine days before Christmas. Children play a game in which they are blindfolded and then take turns using a stick to try to break the piñata, which hangs above their heads. After it breaks, participants scramble to collect the goodies that spill out. Ask children to describe other games they enjoy playing at birthday parties or other kinds of family celebrations.

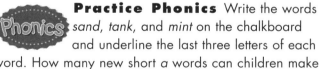

ASSESSMENT

The checked questions on the opposite page help assess children's understanding of:

✔ the **theme** of what our actions tell about us.

✔ the **key strategy** of Make Predictions.

✔ how **comparing** and **contrasting** characters helps readers understand the story.

Practice Phonics Write the words *sand, tank,* and *mint* on the chalkboard and underline the last three letters of each word. How many new short *a* words can children make with the phonograms *and* and *ank*? How many short *i* words can they make with the phonogram *int*? Have children use each of the words they make in a sentence.

Listen to Children Read Ask children to turn to their favorite page and let them read it aloud. You may wish to tape-record their readings.

Children may add their recordings, their completed Story Organizer, and other completed work to their Literacy Portfolios.

Writing

"When I was growing up, my great-aunt, Ygnacia Delgado, was one of my favorite people. Over the years I found that she has become the inspiration for a number of poems and stories I have written. I dedicated *A Birthday Basket for Tía* to the memory of my dear Tía Ygnacia and to all the aunts and great-aunts who surprise us with their love."

Pat Mora

IDEAS FOR WRITING

Picture Book

Ask children to imagine a surprise party that Tía plans for Cecilia. Have them answer these questions:

◆ Who would come to the party? What games would they play? What food would be served? What gift would Tía give to Cecilia?

Then give each child several sheets of drawing paper. Have children draw pictures to show the different things that happen at Cecilia's party. Under each picture, have them write a sentence that tells what is happening. Let children create a cover for their picture book. It can have an illustration and the title *A Birthday Party for Cecilia*. Encourage children to share their picture books with the class.

Thank-You Note

Have children write a thank-you note from Tía to Cecilia for the basket. Encourage children to write the date, a greeting, and a closing.

Personal Story

Invite children to write about a special time they have spent with a favorite relative or another older person. Encourage children to describe what they did and what made it so special. If possible have children bring in photographs that show them together on that special day.

A Poem for Tía

Have children make a birthday card that Cecilia might have made for Tía Rosa. Ask them to create a special picture for the cover of their cards. Then have them write a special message inside in the form of a poem. To get them started you might suggest that they adapt a familiar rhyme to create their poems. For example:

Roses are red.
Violets are blue.
We have fun together.
I love you!

Activities

INTEGRATING LANGUAGE ARTS

Writing/Speaking/Listening

A Birthday Song Invite children to write a song for Cecilia to sing to Tía at her surprise party. It might be sung to the tune of "Happy Birthday" or another popular song. In the song, Cecilia could tell why she loves Tía, or how she feels about Tía's ninetieth birthday. Volunteers can perform their songs or record them for the class to hear.

Speaking/Listening

In Tía's Basket Have children sit in a circle and play the following game:

1. One child begins by naming an item to put in Tía's basket. For example: "In Tía's basket I would put an apple."

2. The next child repeats the previous item and then adds another. For example: "In Tía's basket I would put an apple and a ring."

3. The third child repeats the previous two items and then adds another.

4. Play continues until everyone in the circle has participated. If players cannot recall an item during their turn, a volunteer may help.

INTEGRATING THE CURRICULUM

The Arts

Crafts Cecilia works hard to create the perfect birthday present for Tía. Challenge children to make an original gift for a friend or family member. When deciding on the present, they should consider the person's interests, needs, and favorite colors. You might suggest gifts such as these:

bookmark	picture frame	name tag
paper hat	pencil holder	birthday card

Later, hold a crafts fair. Let children display their individual items and explain how they made them.

Social Studies

Interview Tía tells Cecilia what she did in Mexico when she was a little girl. Encourage children to interview an older family member or neighbor to learn about their childhood. Have them prepare questions such as the following:

◆ What city or country did you grow up in?

◆ How were things different than they are now?

◆ How did you celebrate birthdays or holidays?

Have children take notes on the answers they receive, or tape record them. Later, invite children to share their information with the class.

Story Organizer

Fill in the boxes. Use clues from the story and what you know.

PREDICTION CHART

Clues From the Story

What I Know

Prediction